LITTLE MISS TIDY

Roger Hargreaves

Original
Roger Hargreaves

EGMONT

Little Miss Tidy was an extraordinarily tidy person.

In Little Miss Tidy's house everything had its place.

She had a huge handbag.

Which she would fill with all sorts of things until she had time to put them away tidily.

Then there were all her boxes.

She had
small ones,
medium-sized ones,
big ones,
enormous ones,
round ones,
and square ones.

And this was where Little Miss Tidy tidied away
all her things.

Nothing was ever left lying around in her house.

Now, with all this tidying up going on, you would think that Little Miss Tidy was perfect, wouldn't you?

Well, she isn't!

On Monday at nine o'clock she telephoned Mr Clever.

"As you are so clever," she said, "could you tell me where I put my hairbrush when I tidied up?"

On Tuesday at ten o'clock she telephoned Mr Mean.

"As you like money so much," she said, "could you tell me where I put my purse when I tidied up?"

On Wednesday at eleven o'clock she telephoned Mr Strong.

"As you like eggs so much," she said, "could you tell me where I put my boiled egg when I tidied up?"

On Thursday at twelve o'clock she telephoned
Mr Nosey.

"As you are always poking your nose into things," she
said, "could you tell me where I put my serving spoon
when I tidied up?"

On Friday she didn't telephone anybody because she had tidied away her telephone, and she had to run all the way to Little Miss Chatterbox's house.

"As you love using the telephone," she said, "could you tell me where I put my telephone when I tidied up?"

Luckily, thanks to her friends, Little Miss Tidy was able to find all the things she had lost that week.

Her hairbrush was in a glovebox.

Her purse was in a shoebox.

Her boiled egg was in the salt pot.

Her serving spoon was in the toolbox.

And her telephone was in her sewing box.

Little Miss Tidy certainly was very absent-minded when it came to remembering where she had put things when she was tidying up.

But she couldn't help it.

On Saturday it was her birthday, and Little Miss Chatterbox came to her house, carrying a splendid-looking parcel all tied up with red ribbon.

Little Miss Tidy couldn't wait to see what was inside the present.

It was a notebook and pencil.

The perfect present for somebody who lost things as easily as Little Miss Tidy.

Little Miss Tidy was as happy as … well, as happy as Mr Happy.

She spent the rest of the day opening all her boxes and writing down in her notebook everything that she had stored away in them.

It was very late by the time she had finished her list.

She went to bed, very tired.

On Sunday morning she woke with a start.

"My notebook and pencil!" she cried.

"Where ever did I put them when I tidied up?"

Little Miss Tidy spent all day Sunday looking for her notebook and pencil.

She had to open and close all her boxes again.

And do you know where she eventually found her notebook and pencil?

On her bedside table!